LOOK AND FIND®

Disney · PIXAR
RATATOUILLE
(rat·a·too·ee)

Illustrated by Art Mawhinney and the Disney Storybook Artists
Inspired by the art and character designs created by Pixar

Disney/Pixar elements © Disney/Pixar

This publication may not be reproduced in whole or in part by any
means whatsoever without written permission from the copyright owners.
Permission is never granted for commercial purposes.

Published by Louis Weber, C.E.O.
Publications International, Ltd.
7373 North Cicero Avenue, Lincolnwood, Illinois 60712
Ground Floor, 59 Gloucester Place, London W1U 8JJ

Customer Service: 1-800-595-8484
or customer_service@pilbooks.com

www.pilbooks.com

Manufactured in USA.

p i kids is a registered trademark
of Publications International, Ltd.
Look and Find is a registered trademark
of Publications International, Ltd.,
in the United States and in Canada.

8 7 6 5 4 3 2 1

ISBN-13: 978-1-4127-6837-5
ISBN-10: 1-4127-6837-3

Here we are in the French countryside. The sun is shining and the rats are hungry. Remy, the rat with the keenest nose, must sniff each bit of food to make sure it isn't poisoned. But Remy doesn't care for most of the food brought by the other rats. Look for these unsavory morsels.

Fish bones

Old grapes

Melon rind

Apple core

Potato peel

Drumstick

Candy bar

Remy discovers he is in the elegant city of Paris, near Gusteau's restaurant. High above the bustling streets, Remy looks down on all the metropolis has to offer. Look for these food-related shops that might excite Remy.

CAFÉ

CHOCOLATIER

BRASSERIE

CHARCUTERIE

TRAITEUR

PATISSERIE

La Boulangerie

Inspired by the busy kitchen at Gusteau's, Remy has decided to fix a savory soup. As his delicious pot simmers on the stove, look for these various kitchen utensils that gourmet chefs keep around a well-stocked kitchen.

Rolling pin

Mandolin

Salt cellar

Bread knife

Cheese knife

Mezzaluna

Hoping he can make the young man into a chef, Remy has come to Linguini's apartment for a quick course in culinary competence. While the capable rodent guides his blindfolded pupil, look around the apartment for some of Linguini's belongings.

Soda can

Bike

Running shoes

Soccer ball

Comic book

Cereal box

Tennis racket

Remy has returned! Reunited with his father, Django, and the rest of the rat colony, Remy finds himself in the middle of a celebration. Look around the sewer party for these rat-band members and their musical instruments.

Drinking-straw flute

Paper-clip harp

Nut-shell violin

Salt-shaker maraca

Homemade horn

Rubber-band bass fiddle

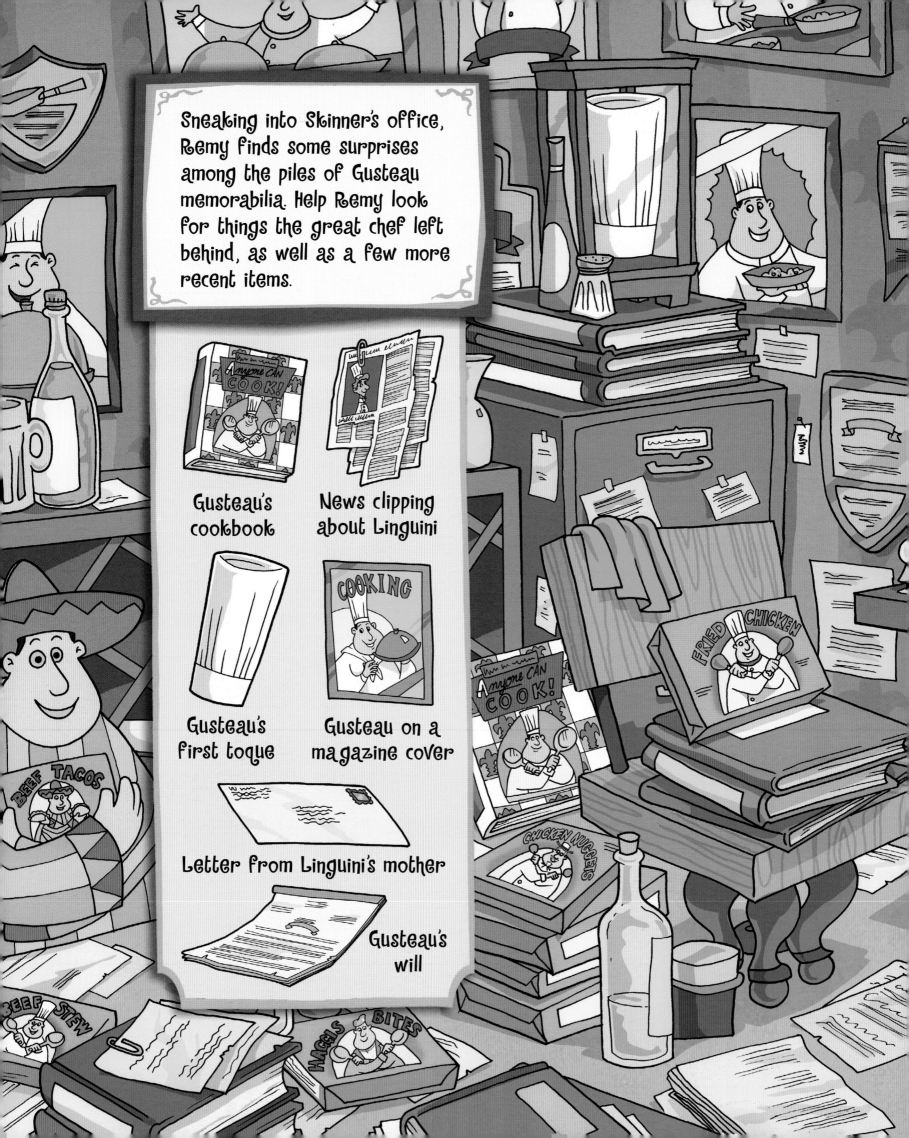

Sneaking into Skinner's office, Remy finds some surprises among the piles of Gusteau memorabilia. Help Remy look for things the great chef left behind, as well as a few more recent items.

Gusteau's cookbook

News clipping about Linguini

Gusteau's first toque

Gusteau on a magazine cover

Letter from Linguini's mother

Gusteau's will

Linguini opens the door to the restaurant's walk-in refrigerator to find a surprise-rats! Emile has led the entire colony to Gusteau's, and now they are stealing all the food they can get their paws on. Look through the shelves of food to find these rats.

It is time for Linguini's big test! He must flabbergast the fussy taste buds of the famed food critic Ego. Look around the dining room of Gusteau's for these fine foods that are being served.

Prawns

Cheese plate

Pâté

Fancy vegetable dish

Leg of lamb

Chocolate mousse

File back to the food line in the countryside to find these foods that Remy would enjoy eating.

Petit four

Soufflé

Brie

Canapé

Truffle oil

Baguette

Escargot

Make your way back to Gusteau's kitchen and find these ingredients that went into Remy's soup.

Rosemary

Onion

Bay leaves

Red peppers

Basil

Chicken stock

Head back to Paris and find these different bicycles that cruise the busy streets.

Red bicycle
Pink bicycle
Purple bicycle

Blue bicycle
Green bicycle
Yellow bicycle

Stumble back through Linguini's apartment to find these cooking utensils.

Whisk

Garlic press

Frying pan

Grater

Potato peeler

Butcher knife

Cutting board

Sneak into the sewers of Paris to find these things the rats have gathered to decorate their new home.

Matchbook
Sardine tin
Fork

Bottle cap
Shoelace
Boot

Creep back into Skinner's office and look for these foods being sold under Gusteau's famous name.

Haggis bites

Chicken nuggets

Corn dogs

BBQ meat

Burritos

Fried chicken

Step back into the walk-in refrigerator at Gusteau's to look for these fine foods.

Caviar

Cheese wheel

Grapes

Lobster

Rib eye steaks

Fine chocolates

Sit back down in Gusteau's dining room and find...

Remy

Linguini's roller skates

Ego

Colette

Skinner in disguise

Pot of ratatouille